The Adventur

Alexander Elliot

Written by Kathryn Sherry

Illustrated by Cristal Baldwin

THE ADVENTURES OF ALEXANDER ELLIOTT

First Old Scout Press Edition July 2019

Old Scout Press
Charlotte, NC

www.OldScoutPress.com

ISBN: 978-0-578-54238-6

Book design by Meredith Ray

1   3   5   7   9   10   8   6   4   2

For Bryan...my favorite adventure.

Alexander Elliott loves adventure.

Sea monsters, pirates, dinosaur fossils, tractor racing, space exploration...he loves reading about it all.

He also has a big imagination and loves to look for adventure, just like the characters in the stories he reads.

Most of his favorite adventure-seeking characters wear something distinctive like a mask or a hat.

For Alexander Elliott, he wears a special red cape.

He made it out of
one of his Dad's old
turtlenecks.

His dog, Duke, wears a red cape as well.
Except his is much smaller.

Once that cape is on, Alexander Elliott's imagination goes wild and any adventure is possible!

When Mom says, "It's time to clean your room," his floor magically transforms into bubbling hot lava and both Alexander Elliott and Duke have to jump on the furniture so they don't touch the ground.

When Dad says, "Come help me
mow the lawn," suddenly Dad's riding
lawnmower becomes a bucking bronco
entering the Rodeo arena while
Alexander Elliott fearlessly holds on

On Halloween he was allowed to wear a costume to school.
Of course, he wore his red cape.

When his classmate, Charlotte, asked him
what his costume was for Halloween he
told her he was Captain Adventure and
showed her his best superhero pose.

Davis, another student, overheard their conversation.

"What kind of adventures do you go on?" Davis asked curiously.

Alexander Elliott shrugged. "Any adventure you can imagine," he answered.

Davis looked confused.

"Like what?" Another classmate, Emmy, questioned.
Alexander Elliott thought for a moment. He had been on so many exciting
adventures it was difficult to remember them all.

"Well," he began, "like deep-sea diving."

"Or dogsledding through a blizzard."

"Or hang gliding through the air!"

"But where do you find these adventures?" Another student, Arnold, said joining the conversation as well.

At this point, Alexander Elliott realized there was a group of classmates surrounding him all wondering the same thing...how do you find adventure?

Alexander Elliott grinned.

He turned around to search for one of his favorite adventures on the classroom bookshelf. When he finally found it he faced his classmates.

"Adventure is everywhere," he told them as he showed them the cover of the book he had selected. The title read, *Volcano!*

That day, instead of playing Pumpkin Bowling at the Halloween Class Party, Alexander Elliott taught his new friends that nothing was more exciting than the adventures they created with their imaginations.

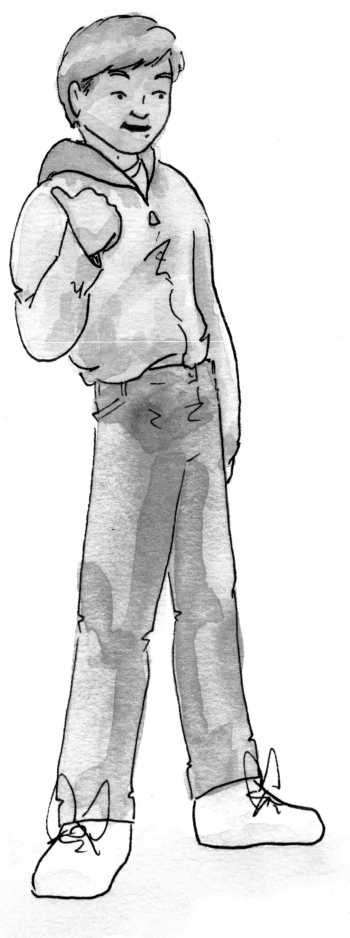

Today as he puts on his
red cape his Dad says,
"Let's go rake some leaves
for you to jump in!"

Normally his weekly autumn chore of raking leaves in the yard would suddenly become a deep forest exploration to find treasure in Mom's enormous sunflower garden.

But today with all the leaves on the ground,
Alexander Elliott spots the perfect tree to climb.

He loves to climb trees.
With his cape on, he imagines that
the tree is actually Mount Everest
and he is bravely climbing his way
to the top of the mountain.

As Alexander Elliott reaches up towards the final branch he suddenly hears a loud sound.

Rrrriiiiiip!

He looks down and notices that his cape is caught on a branch. He tries to yank the cape off but it doesn't budge.

Admitting defeat, Alexander Elliott sadly unties his cape and begins to carefully climb down from the tree.

He thinks of all the ways he could save his cape like the heroes in his adventure stories. Maybe he could chop down the tree like a strong lumberjack.

Perhaps he could parachute from a plane
and snatch it as he floats down.

Or maybe zip line through the trees
and grab the cape as he glides by the branch.

Once on the ground he looks back up at his cape hanging from the branch. The red cape blowing in the wind reminds him of a flag on a castle or a pirate ship.

This gives Alexander Elliott an idea.

He races back to his house to gather some materials and then returns to the tree where the red cape still blows in the wind.

He sets up an old camping tent
(with the help of his Dad, of course).

Inside the tent he places his favorite
adventure books, sleeping bags, a
flashlight, and some tasty snacks
(with the help of his Mom, of course).

Beside the tent he makes a large sign that reads, *The Adventure Club.*

Now everyone would know where to find adventure,
thanks to Alexander Elliott and his flying red cape.

About the Author

Connecticut native, Kathryn Sherry, resides in Charlotte, NC. Her passion for children's literature and writing led to working in publishing in New York and later a return to school to obtain a Masters in Elementary Education. Now in her tenth year of teaching, Kathryn nurtures her kindergarten students' imagination and love of reading every day.

About the Illustrator

Cristal Baldwin is an artist that lives in the small town of London, Ohio. She resides there with her husband, son, a rescue dog, kitty and another rescue cat. They like to sit on her artwork when she is not looking. Cristal received her fine arts degree from Wittenberg University, in Springfield, Ohio, and continues to create a variety of artwork.

www.flyingfrogstudio.net

Made in the USA
Monee, IL
27 September 2019